Dreamy Daisy

and other stories

Hodder
Children's
Books

A division of Hachette Children's Books

How to make your Felicity wishes

WISH

With this book comes an extra special wish
for you and your best friend.

Hold the book together at each end and
both close your eyes.

Wriggle your noses and think of a
number under ten.

Open your eyes, whisper the numbers you
thought of to each other.

Add these numbers together. This is your

Magic Number.

you

best friend

Place your little finger
on the stars, and say your magic number
out loud together. Now make your wish
quietly to yourselves. And maybe, one day,
your wish might just come true.

Love felicity

With extra sparkly wishes
for Bridgit Calthrop

Emma Thomson's
felicity Wishes®

FELICITY WISHES
Felicity Wishes © 2000 Emma Thomson
Licensed by White Lion Publishing

Text and Illustrations © 2006 Emma Thomson

First published in Great Britain in 2006 by Hodder Children's Books

4

A Catalogue record for this book is available from the British Library

ISBN-10: 0 340 91197 2
ISBN-13: 9780340091976

Printed and bound in Great Britain by Bookmarque Ltd, Croydon, Surrey

The paper and board used in this paperback by Hodder Children's Books are natural recyclable
products made from wood grown in sustainable forests. The manufacturing processes
conform to the environmental regulations of the country of origin.

Hodder Children's Books
A division of Hachette Children's Books, 338 Euston Road, London NW1 3BH

CONTENTS

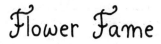

Dreamy Daisy

Daisy was the dreamiest of all Felicity Wishes' friends. She was also the quietest, which meant that if you didn't know she was daydreaming, you'd think she was a very shy fairy.

Daisy daydreamed about most things. She daydreamed about how it came to be that the grass was green and not blue, why fairies could fly and animals couldn't. But mostly, she daydreamed about anything and everything to do with flowers. Flowers were her absolute passion: from the

tiniest seed through to the largest
sunflower, Daisy loved them all.

"Does everyone agree?"
said Felicity loudly.

Holly, Polly and
Winnie whooped
with a resounding
"Yesssss!"

"W-w-what?"
said Daisy, coming
back down to Fairy
World with a bump.

Felicity, Holly, Winnie and Polly
looked at Daisy, mouths wide open.

"How can you say 'what'?" said
Holly, aghast. "We've just spent the
last three days talking about nothing
else but the School of Nine Wishes
disco."

But Daisy had other things on her
mind.

"Daisy, are you up for working out
a dance routine to Susie Sparkle's

new single for the disco?" repeated Felicity patiently.

Daisy looked clueless.

"This evening at my house?" prompted Felicity.

"Oh, no, I can't!" said Daisy, quick as a flash. "I've arranged to meet Miss Briar. We're discussing the floral displays for Little Blossoming's Best Village entry."

Daisy had never been considered qualified enough to help out on the Best Village team before. Being a novice fairy at the School of Nine Wishes meant that she didn't yet have her double wings or, more importantly, a certificate to be a fully qualified Blossom Fairy.

"Why didn't you say anything before?" said Holly, exasperated. "We're a team, and without you our dance routine just won't be the same."

Felicity quickly stepped in. "Don't

worry, Daisy," she said kindly. "We'll work something out."

* * *

Daisy had no problem concentrating in the meeting with Miss Briar that evening. When Daisy thought of flowers it was as if she flowered herself.

"I was thinking," said Daisy tentatively, as she opened her notebook, "of doing something like this!"

Miss Briar took Daisy's outstretched notebook and looked closely at the page.

"It's wonderful!" said Miss Briar. "Truly inspirational."

Daisy blushed a delicate rose pink.

"And you say you've haven't even graduated yet? I can't believe you don't have your double wings!"

Feeling more confident now, Daisy elaborated. "Well, I thought as the prize-giving is going to be held in Little Blossoming, it will be a perfect opportunity to show the judges why they chose us for first prize!"

"You're very confident that we're going to win," said Miss Briar, impressed.

"I know we're going to win, because I know that no one could possibly love flowers as much as I do!" burst out Daisy.

"Well," said Miss Briar, scanning Daisy's plans again. "These drawings look out of this world. But is that because they are out of this world?"

Daisy looked puzzled.

"What I mean is," continued Miss Briar, "are they achievable? We only have a month until the competition."

Daisy turned the page. "I've been looking on the World Wide Wand," she said. "I was waiting to see what you said before I went any further, but I've already found lots of eager flower growers and professional Blossom Fairies from around the world who are interested in helping!"

Miss Briar quickly scanned the list.

"Well, Daisy, it appears as though you've got yourself a job! You will be in charge of decorating the prize-giving garden and throwing a garden party fit for a fairy queen, to be ready no later than four weeks from today."

✳ ✳ ✳

Over the next few days at school Felicity, Holly, Winnie and Polly hardly saw their flowery friend and they missed her very much.

"How can we do a five-fold flip if there are just four of us?" sighed Winnie in exasperation, as they tried in vain to practise their dance routine.

"I've promised to teach Daisy the steps after school today at her house," said Felicity. "Don't worry, she won't let us down. Everything will be all right on the night!"

* * *

But when Felicity got to Daisy's house that evening there was no one in.

Instead there was a note written in rushed handwriting pinned to the front door.

Felicity, sorry, I had to go. One and only chance to collect magical seeds to make sure Little Blossoming wins the Best Village prize. See you at school tomorrow. Daisy x

And while Felicity headed back home, Daisy was winging her way to the other side of the country. The landscape changed from familiar trees and open countryside to larger towns and cities, until the sky grew dark. Usually Daisy didn't like to travel too far from home as most of her flowers needed constant care, but this trip was vital if she was to have any chance of winning the competition.

Daisy had found the advert for the magical seeds in a free magazine that had been posted through her letter box. It was the type of magazine that most sensible fairies ignored. Daisy had pored over it, dreamily visualizing all the magical contraptions that sceptical fairies knew would never work in a million fairy years.

As Daisy flew she began to imagine

Miss Magic's Magazine

TWINKLE TOES!

Why have a pair of slippers and spend good wishing time wondering where you put them when you can have one **giant** slipper that's so big you'll never have to hunt it down.

WRONG WISH EXTRACTOR

Made a mistake with your wish? Suck it back before it works with this wonderful wrong wish extractor.

The Amazing WANDHANDLEWARMER

Fed up freezing your fingers on frosty mornings? Make every day toasty in winter with this handy pouch. You'll 'wand'er what you did without it!

Marvellous carpet seeds

SPECIAL OFFER

Make your garden the spectacular outside room you've always wanted. Watch a veritable feast of floral patterns unfold before your very eyes! Perfect for parties and other large events. Available in five different patterns.

Hand held wand fan

Fed up flying in the heat? Need a constant breeze to help you keep your cool? With this **super fantastic** spinning star wand, clammy days are in the past.

Miss Magic's house. She hoped it would be surrounded by colourful carpets of flowers so she could see what her prize-winning area would look like.

"Miss Magic might even invite me in for a cup of chamomile tea after my long trip," she thought.

But when she finally turned on to the road given in the address on the advert, Daisy became confused. Before her stretched a row of large and looming warehouses. Squinting into the dark as she fluttered up the road, she passed warehouse after warehouse, searching for number fifty-one. Tentatively she pressed the intercom buzzer.

"Um, hello, I was wondering if you could help me. I'm looking for Miss Magic's house and I'm afraid I'm in the wrong town entirely."

"Oh, no," said a gruff voice, "you've

got the right place. Push the door
when the buzzer sounds."

* * *

The next day at school, Felicity, Holly,
Polly and Winnie could see that their
friend was tired.

"Dreaming about your prize-winning
floral display again?" said Felicity,
gently nudging her friend awake.

"Wha-what?" said Daisy, unsure of
where she was. "I was up all last night
planting seeds," she said with a big

yawn. "I won't know the results for a week, but if the picture is anything to go by they're going to blow the judges' wings away!"

"Are they special seeds then?" asked Polly, eager to show an interest.

Daisy handed her friends the advert.

"Oh, Daisy," said Holly, not able to help herself. All the fairy friends knew Daisy was sometimes a little gullible, and they didn't like to see her set her hopes high on something so ridiculous.

Felicity struggled for something to say. "This looks beautiful, but it might be worth thinking of a Plan B, just in case this doesn't work out."

"Oh, this will work," Daisy said resolutely. "The fairy in the importing warehouse gave Miss Magic's personal guarantee."

Daisy's friends raised their eyes to the sky.

* * *

The next week, Daisy was on her way
back from watering her seeds when
she bumped into her four best fairy
friends flying towards her with armfuls
of lavender, honeysuckle, jasmine and
orange-blossom plants.

"Surprise!" said Felicity, landing
with a fairylike bump and planting
an armful of pots in Daisy's arms.

"Thanks!" said Daisy, a little
confused.

"We thought we'd give you some
help with your Plan B, just in case
your Plan A doesn't work," said Holly
tactlessly.

"Miss Briar has every confidence that I can come up with the results," said Daisy, a little offended. "Thank you, though. I can plant these along with the flowers the professional gardeners are growing for the borders."

* * *

That night, Daisy went to bed a very happy fairy. Everything was coming together beautifully. The seeds had begun to germinate under the sheet. In three or four days they would be strong enough to flower, in perfect time for the judging and prize-giving day. The professional gardeners had started to send in their flowers, and now with her friends' extra flowers it was going to be better than ever.

"Miss Briar will be so proud," thought Daisy happily to herself as she slipped into a sweet floral dream.

* * *

The next day at school Daisy had an announcement for her friends. "I know I've been in a bit of a daydream recently."

Holly raised her eyebrows and giggled.

"OK, I know I've been in even more of a daydream recently," said Daisy, laughing. "But everything is under control now and I'd really like to spend some time learning the dance routine for the school disco!"

Felicity, Holly, Polly and Winnie hugged Daisy all at once.

✳ ✳ ✳

After school they spent hours practising, giggling while Daisy learnt the steps her friends now knew off by heart.

"Hovering in the air like this for the whole routine is so different!" said Daisy, flapping her wings at double speed.

"That's why it's called the Hover-hop!" shouted Holly above Susie Sparkle's music.

"Once you start you can't stop!"

"We're going to be the talk of the disco!" said Daisy, beaming.

"And you're going to be the talk of the town when everyone sees your fantastic floral display," said Felicity, tapping her toe to the beat of the music. "How's it going, by the way?"

Holly stopped hovering, turned down the music and joined Felicity, Winnie and Polly as they stood anxiously waiting for Daisy to reply.

"Oh, great!" Daisy said, shocking them all. "Most of the buds have begun to open. If you like, you can have a sneak preview before the show."

"We'd love to!" they said in unison, the relief on their faces plain to see.

* * *

Three days later the Best Village judging day had arrived. Daisy had been awake since four a.m.; she could barely wait to peel back the large protective sheeting to reveal the wonderful floral carpet she had so carefully tended.

When Felicity, Holly, Polly and Winnie arrived at the walled garden

that contained the judging area, there
was already a throng of fairies waiting
to get in. As they shuffled their way to
the front, Daisy was waiting for them.
She opened the large wooden gate and
quickly squeezed her friends inside.

Felicity, Holly, Polly and Winnie
were speechless. The carpet of flowers
had burst into bloom in the most

intricate and awe-inspiring pattern. None of the fairies had ever seen anything like it before.

"It's stunning," said Felicity, giving her friend an extra-special hug.

"And look!" said Winnie proudly. "Our lavender, jasmine and orange-blossom plants look wonderful surrounding the edge like that!"

"The fairies queuing up outside are going to love it!" said Polly.

"But it's the judges I need to impress most," said Daisy, nervously twirling a curl of her hair.

Then suddenly Felicity had a thought. "What entertainment are you putting on for the garden party then?" she said, still admiring the garden.

Daisy's smile suddenly turned to shock. "Oh, my goodness!" she said, putting her hand up to her mouth. "I was so busy concentrating on the flower display, I completely forgot about the entertainment! Oh, no, it's a disaster! Little Blossoming will never win now and it will all be my fault."

Suddenly Felicity flew into the middle of the garden and began to dance the routine they had made up for the School of Nine Wishes disco.

"This is no time for dancing!" said Polly sharply.

"I'm not just dancing!" said Felicity, flying over and pulling all her friends into the centre of the garden. "I'm helping Daisy throw a garden party!"

As Felicity and her friends wiggled their hips and flapped their wings, they also helped release the smell of all the wonderful scented flowers in the display. So not only did the garden look beautiful, it smelt beautiful too.

* * *

When Daisy flew up to the podium to collect the first prize on behalf of Little

Blossoming, the judges all lined up
to congratulate her personally.

"Wonderful!" said one.

"I will remember the smell of the
flowers for eternity," said another.

"A magical and unique idea – a
breathtaking floral display with its
very own personalized dance routine.
Can I ask what inspired you?"

"Friends!" said Daisy, pulling Felicity
and the others on to the podium. "I
couldn't have done it without them!"

Anything is po...

...with a ...help from
your friends

Flo

"I expect th
plants th
"Oh
ho

"It all began when I won the Best
Village award with my fragrant floral
display," said Daisy to the reporter.

Daisy was a floral celebrity! She had
almost lost her shy and quiet nature.

The reporter pushed her tape
recorder a little closer towards Daisy.
"I did hear that you were the first to
start off the amazing craze for flowers
that has swept Fairy World."

"Yes," agreed Daisy. "I had a letter
from someone the other day from
Bird Island who wanted my tips for
her own village green."

ey have slightly different
re," said the reporter.
, yes," said Daisy eagerly. "I still
ve so much to learn."

"I was told that you're still a novice
fairy at school. I can see by your single
wings that that is correct."

Daisy looked sheepish. She was so
anxious to be taken seriously, but until
she graduated to a full pair of double
wings it was going to be very difficult,
no matter how many garden awards
she won.

"Yes. Being at school is sometimes
hard, when all I really want to do is
spend all my time with flowers. I have
my holidays though, and this summer
I'm going to travel to discover new
and exotic species."

* * *

"Can we come too?" asked Felicity,
when she learnt about Daisy's trip.

"I'd love to say yes," said Daisy. "But

it might be dangerous, and I wouldn't want to put any of you at risk."

"Even more reason for someone to go with you," said Winnie. "I'd love to come, but I promised I'd help with the school trip."

Felicity snuggled up to Daisy on the Sparkles Café couch. "It's always good to have company if you're off on an adventure!"

"Oh, OK!" said Daisy, giving in. "As long as no one else gets jealous!"

"We won't if you send us a postcard and bring us back presents!" said Holly.

* * *

The trip took a lot of planning. Daisy never usually liked to travel far from home because of the precious plants in her garden that needed constant care and attention. But with Winnie, Holly and Polly staying in Little Blossoming she knew her garden's needs would be in safe hands. Well, with Polly at least!

Daisy and Felicity planned to go to the far north of Fairy World. In summer it was daylight for a full twenty-four hours. It never got dark, even at night. This meant that there were

species of plants that couldn't possibly grow anywhere else.

For Felicity it was the chance for an adventure beyond her wildest dreams. Most of the rare flowers could only be found on the path leading to the top

of one of the highest mountains in
Fairy World.

* * *

"You've changed!" said Felicity,
nestling back in her aeroplane seat.

Daisy looked doubtfully at Felicity
as she handed back an autograph to
an eager fairy.

"Honestly, you have!" Felicity said.
"When I first met you, you were so shy
and dreamy, and now look at you!
You've got fans everywhere you go."

Daisy blushed. "I'm still the same
fairy underneath. All of this, it won't
last, but the flowers will. And as long
as I am as true to them as they are to
me, I will be happy for ever."

* * *

The country at the top of Fairy World
is called Warm Glow. Its landscape
is very similar to parts of Little
Blossoming, but the weather is entirely
different. With twenty-four hours of

sunshine, its warmth made the fairies' wings tingle when they got off the plane.

Once they had settled into their hotel, Daisy and Felicity went for a cool drink in the restaurant. Felicity was desperately trying to work out a route up the mountain that would pass all the possible sites for flowers.

"If only Winnie was here to help," she sighed, trying to work out which way was north. Geography was never her strongest subject at school.

"Excuse me!" called a fairy from the other side of the restaurant. "I was told you might be here! Is it really you? I've loved your garden displays for ever! Can I have your autograph?" and she got up and started to fly towards Daisy and Felicity's table.

"Is there nowhere you're not known in Fairy World?" giggled Felicity.

Embarrassed by the attention, Daisy

began to get up to greet the fairy, but to her surprise she flew straight past and on to a table behind them.

"You're the most famous Blossom Fairy in the whole of Fairy World," gushed the admiring fairy to someone at the other table. "I hope you don't mind my asking. I have a copy of your book here. If you'd dedicate it to Suzy that would make my day!"

Straining to overhear the conversation, Daisy and Felicity leant back in their seats.

"I'd be pleased to," said the fairy voice. "I've come all this way to climb up magical Mount Stamen and bring back something that will hopefully make me more famous than this book ever did! I'm going to start an exotic flower emporium!"

"How exciting, Professor Gushing," said Suzy.

Daisy and Felicity exchanged looks. Daisy herself had all Professor Gushing's books, although she'd never seen her before. The professor was well known not only for her amazing garden displays, but also for having discovered and cultivated most of the amazing plants available in garden centres all over Fairy World.

* * *

The next day at breakfast, Daisy eyed Professor Gushing covertly from behind her newspaper.

"Why don't you just go and say hello?" asked Felicity.

"I'm shy!" said Daisy. "She's such a heroine of mine, I'd probably just end up saying something silly and making a fool of myself. Anyway, she's going now, look."

Felicity turned to see Professor Gushing heave on an enormous rucksack and hug well-wishers goodbye.

Felicity and Daisy weren't ready for their journey until much later that morning. Felicity had spent hours filling every available space in her bag with fruit fizzes and liquorice laces to keep her going on the trek.

Unlike Felicity, Daisy had spent her time carefully preparing the essential tools for the trip ahead. She had no idea what flowers she might or might not find but she had made sure she had dozens of seed-collecting tools,

and little brown envelopes to
catalogue them all.

* * *

To Felicity's surprise the base of the
mountain was barren. Most of the
land was deep-red earth in which
nothing whatsoever grew.

"Are you sure we're in the right
place?" asked Felicity.

Daisy nodded earnestly. "Most of the
flowers won't start to appear until we
are at least a quarter of the way up."

"Let's hope we find some
flowers before bedtime
then," said Felicity,
looking quizzically
at her map.

There was a long way to go and
Felicity wasn't used to walking further
than Star Street for a shopping spree.

* * *

The path that made its way up the
first part of the mountain was easy,
if a little rocky. The red soil soon
gave way to hard stones and Felicity
was pleased that Daisy had made
her wear sensible walking boots.

The views that surrounded them
showed other similar mountains all
around. There wasn't a house in
sight.

"I bet the sunset will be incredible!"
said Felicity, stopping for a moment
to catch her breath and take in her
surroundings.

"There are no sunsets, remember!"
said Daisy. "We're so far north the
sun never sets. That's why the hotel
has such heavy curtains!"

* * *

By the time they stopped for some late lunch, the fairy friends had made good progress.

"I thought we might have seen some flowers by now," said Daisy, leaning back on the picnic rug and inspecting the shrubs that now surrounded them.

"That's funny," she said, suddenly getting closer to the green leaves and consulting one of her reference books.

"I thought they were familiar. These leaves are very similar to the Star

Flower leaves you can find in Nine Wish Wood. If they're of the same family it says here they should be flowering by now, but there are no flowers. There aren't even any buds."

∗ ∗ ∗

Daisy and Felicity didn't have much more luck for the rest of that afternoon. Even though the ground around them had gradually become more green and lush, there was no sign of any flowers.

"I don't understand," said Felicity, heading in a new direction. "There are flowers over here, away from the path."

Daisy looked desperately at the pretty dots of colour she could just make out in the distance. "No," she said, "we mustn't stray from the path. It's too dangerous. We must press on."

"But it's nearly bedtime and my feet

are aching after all this walking,"
said Felicity, rubbing her tired feet.
"Can't we stop here and set up camp?"

"Just a little bit longer," persuaded
Daisy.

* * *

And because it didn't get dark and
each corner they turned looked much
the same as the last, the fairies lost
track of time.

"Oh, my goodness," said Daisy with
a sudden shriek. "It's one in the
morning!"

"Please can we go to bed now?"
begged Felicity, unable to go any
further. "And perhaps," she said
tentatively, "after we've slept we
should just give up and go back to
the hotel. There are other mountains."

"We can't possibly!" said Daisy,
tears welling up in her eyes. "This is
the mountain for flowers, it's world-
renowned. What kind of Blossom

Fairy am I trying to be if I can't find any flowers here?"

Felicity knew Daisy was tired and both of them were hungry.

"Let's set up camp, have something to eat, and in the morning we can decide what to do. Look, there's a nice flat clearing just around the corner."

As they turned the corner Daisy and Felicity couldn't believe their eyes.

There in the middle of the grass was a one-fairy tent, and surrounding it were dozens and dozens of vases full of flowers.

Daisy knew immediately whom the tent belonged to and why they hadn't found any flowers so far.

"How horrid!" whispered Daisy, shocked and upset all at once. "Professor Gushing must have uprooted every single flower from the mountain path on her way up here!"

Felicity didn't know what to say.

"Poor, poor flowers," said Daisy quietly, kneeling by the vases and touching the flowers' delicate petals. "Every good Blossom Fairy knows that you shouldn't take something that can't be replaced. You must be true to flowers, and they will be true to you."

"Maybe Professor Gushing is going to replace them," said Felicity, finding it hard to believe that any fairy would ever do anything knowingly bad.

"Remember what we heard her say to the fairy wanting her autograph. She said that she was going to bring back something to start an exotic plant emporium. I presumed she meant to cultivate the plants from seeds, but seeing this, I know she intends to take the flowers themselves – or she wouldn't have uprooted them."

Suddenly there was a loud snore from inside the tent that made Daisy jump.

"I've got an idea," she said. "But we've got to be quick. What time is it now?"

"It's almost two in the morning," yawned Felicity.

* * *

Daisy and Felicity slept for over twelve hours when they got back to the hotel at eight a.m. that morning. When they woke up, it was time for supper!

"I'm glad we are going home," said Daisy. "I want to get my body clock back to normal."

Just then they heard an enormous commotion in reception.

"I think Professor Gushing has just got back!" said Felicity, giggling, and they quickly made their way downstairs.

"Speechless!" Professor Gushing boomed. "Incredible!" she shouted at the arc of fairies that were watching her in awe. "I know Mount Stamen is called magical, but I had no idea it

was as magical as I found it to be!"

"Look!" she burst out. She threw off her rucksack dramatically, delved into the large front pocket and scattered dozens of small brown packets across the tabletop. "It did this!" she declared in disbelief. "Incredible!" she said again.

"I don't understand," said the receptionist as she picked up an envelope. "I thought you were going up the mountain to take samples to start a new exotic emporium, and isn't that what these brown packets are? Seeds from each of the flowers?"

Professor Gushing looked sheepish and lowered her voice.

"I wasn't going to tell you the full story, but you're right. A good Blossom Fairy would have collected, catalogued and packaged up the seeds, just like this. However, I have been doing this a long time, and over time I have become a little, how shall I say... lazy," she admitted to the crowd.

"Instead of collecting seeds I gathered all the plants themselves. It's much quicker, but I'm afraid it's not really very good for the plants. They never see their home again."

Shocked gasps fell out of open-mouthed fairies.

"But when I woke up this morning,

the mountain had done this!" and Professor Gushing swept her hand over the packets. "There must be secret mountain fairies working up there! Not only had they taken seed samples from each variety for me, but as I made my way back down the mountain I found that they had even replanted each and every flower I had uprooted."

None of the fairies looking on knew what to say or even whether to believe Professor Gushing. They had never heard of any mountain fairies on Mount Stamen before.

Quietly, Daisy shuffled her way to the front.

"So, Professor Gushing," she ventured. "Do you think you will ever uproot a flower again?"

"Oh, no!" said Professor Gushing. "The most important lesson a Blossom Fairy can learn is to be as true to flowers as they are to you, and after this I won't ever forget it again."

* * *

On their return to Little Blossoming, Daisy had an extra-special present for each of her fairy friends.

"Exotic flowers, grown from seeds collected from magical Mount Stamen," she said.

"Yes," giggled Felicity. "A very special mountain with a very special secret!"

Be as true to the
things you love

as they are to you

Exotic Emporium

Daisy had been dreaming. It was such a realistic dream that when she woke up she wondered whether it was in fact real.

"Why don't you make it real?" ventured Felicity, after Daisy had told her all about it in gardening class.

"But it was only a dream," said Daisy.

"I know," said Felicity, "but if you really believe in dreams, you can make them real."

Daisy thought for a moment. "Oh, it will never work."

"That is why you have to believe," said Felicity knowingly. "It will work, if you really believe."

* * *

Daisy had dreamt that she was floating on a cloud of petals, with happiness in her heart like she'd never known before. But as much as she tried, she couldn't think of a single way that she would ever be able to float on a cloud of petals, or feel that impossibly happy. It would have to remain a dream.

* * *

"Fairy World calling Daisy!" said Holly, nudging her friend. "Fairy World calling Daisy!" she repeated.

"Sorry," apologized Daisy. "I was just thinking. What were you saying?"

"I was saying how exciting it is that you're going to stay with Professor

Gushing at Floral Castle. I hear it has flowers in the gardens that have never been seen anywhere else."

"I know," said Daisy, who didn't look very excited.

"What's up?" asked Polly, picking up on her friend's uncertain look.

"Oh, I'm just a little nervous, that's all," said Daisy, looking around at all the wonderful and exotic flowers that surrounded them in the classroom.

"I expect you are," said Felicity. "It's not every day that a trainee fairy is asked to spend time with one of the most experienced Blossom Fairies in Fairy World."

* * *

Daisy had met Professor Gushing at magical Mount Stamen when she and Felicity had gone on a flower expedition. And now Professor Gushing had asked Daisy to attend a special course at her home. In return for letting Daisy out of school, Professor Gushing had promised Fairy Godmother to give a talk to the school about her exotic flower emporium.

"It's just that we didn't exactly get off on the right foot when we met last time," said Daisy, whispering to her friends. "And there are some things I'd rather Professor Gushing didn't see."

Felicity knew exactly what she meant. "Professor Gushing thinks that she is the only fairy who has seeds from Mount Stamen, but Daisy and I collected some too, which are flowering beautifully," she said to her friends, waving her wand across the flowers that surrounded them.

* * *

When Daisy arrived at Floral Castle for the first day of her special course, it was exactly as she'd imagined. The castle was enormous, covered in ivy and the prettiest roses Daisy had ever seen. There were enough rooms for at least a hundred fairies to live there, but Daisy knew that Professor Gushing lived alone, except for her assistant, Persephone.

"Professor Gushing!" said Daisy, smiling at the familiar fairy who opened the large wooden door.

"Daisy!" said Professor Gushing warmly. "It is nice to see you again. Come in, come in! How was your journey? Did you enjoy the trip? Can I carry your bags?"

Daisy didn't know which question to answer first. She'd thought they might not have anything to talk about, but she soon realized that wouldn't be a problem.

"Your room is up here," said the professor, waving her wand towards a spectacular wooden staircase that seemed to go up for ever. "It's one of the best rooms in the house, because it has a magnificent view over my beautiful garden."

Daisy and the professor began to climb the stairs with the heavy bags.

"My assistant, Persephone, would

normally help, but she's... gone away... on holiday," said the professor nervously.

"Who are all these fairies?" said Daisy, looking up at the giant ornate oil masterpieces that lined the walls.

"They are my ancestors," said Professor Gushing. "All of them have moved on now, but each and every one was a renowned Blossom Fairy and lived here in Floral Castle."

Daisy tipped her head back to see some more and nearly tumbled down the stairs.

"That's Petulia, my great-great-great-aunt," said the professor. "She was responsible for discovering the snowdrop in all its different varieties. There are thousands."

"I know," said Daisy in awe. "I have a book just about snowdrops that I keep by my bed. I count them instead of sheep and they help me go to sleep!"

Professor Gushing laughed.

"You think I'm silly," said Daisy.

"No," protested Professor Gushing. "Not at all. I'm laughing because I do exactly the same thing!"

And Daisy knew that they would get on wonderfully.

* * *

Once Daisy had unpacked and freshened up, she made a cup of jasmine tea and phoned Felicity to fill her in on the gossip so far. They hadn't been apart long, but already Daisy was missing her best fairy friend.

* * *

Daisy had only been on the phone for an hour when Professor Gushing knocked on her bedroom door and insisted they begin the course at once.

"We only have four days," she said. "And I want to learn as much as I can from you in that time."

Daisy giggled. "Don't you mean you want me to learn as much from you?" she said.

Professor Gushing blushed. "Oh, yes! Did I say I wanted to learn from you? Oh, how silly of me. No, you must learn as much from me as you can, my dear. After all, I am the professional Blossom Fairy and you are the novice!" She turned around and showed Daisy her beautiful pair of double wings.

* * *

Professor Gushing led Daisy into a vast dark room lined with books, pots, seed trays, papers, magazines and clothes. Daisy looked around and had trouble finding a place to sit down.

"Here," said Professor Gushing, sweeping a large pile of papers and a plant off a chair so that they landed with a thud on the floor. "You can sit here! Now, the first thing I have for you to do is a test."

"A test?" asked Daisy, carefully picking up the plant.

"Yes, a test," said Professor Gushing, pulling out a piece of crumpled paper from under a large pile of books. "It will help me find out, erm, what stage you are at, so I don't go over things you already know."

Daisy looked at the list. The questions were very easy and not at all specific. In fact they were questions any normal fairy might ask, not ones she would have expected from a fairy who'd been studying flowers for an eternity.

By the time Daisy had completed the test there wasn't much of the day left, and she was tired from her long journey. So, after a bite to eat, she retired to bed to finish the last chapter of *Flowers through the Ages*.

✳ ✳ ✳

The next morning Daisy had to open

seven doors before she found the breakfast room, where Professor Gushing was waiting for her.

"Now, dear," she said, "what would you like to eat?"

"Um, I don't know," said Daisy, feeling a little embarrassed about being waited on by this eminent Blossom Fairy. "I do like scrambled eggs, but I'm quite happy to make them myself."

"Oh, my dear, I wouldn't hear of it," said Professor Gushing. "Persephone usually cooks, but I'm sure I can scramble us something together!"

It was soon clear that Professor Gushing was one of those multi-talented fairies who could very easily have been a professional cook if she hadn't become a Blossom Fairy.

"When I was coming down the stairs this morning I took another look at those marvellous portraits," said

Daisy, as she finished her delicious breakfast.

Professor Gushing shifted awkwardly in her chair.

"The painting of the fairy sitting amongst the bluebells looks like it has been painted quite recently," continued Daisy, "and the plaque must be wrong because it said 'Professor Gushing', but it wasn't you."

Professor Gushing stood up abruptly and started to clear the breakfast plates.

"No, no, it's not me. It's another Professor Gushing: an old relative, long gone from here now."

"But the painting looked quite recent," said Daisy, confused.

"Oh, artists!" laughed Professor Gushing. "They're always using magical ever-fresh paint. It's amazing, isn't it? Anyway," she said, changing the subject, "I thought today we might do a little experiment with some of the seeds I collected from magical Mount Stamen."

"Oh, yes!" said Daisy, forgetting all about the painting. "I'd love that."

So, after the breakfast things had been tidied away, Daisy and Professor Gushing headed for the garden where the most wonderful wood-framed greenhouse stood in the midst of many exotic shrubs and plants. Daisy had never seen such splendour before, even in books.

"Beautiful, isn't it?" said Professor Gushing, beaming.

But nothing could have prepared Daisy for the wonders she saw inside the greenhouse. Flowers of every colour of the rainbow filled it, with leaves as delicate as snowflakes and as large as trees fighting for space in between. If this was what the normal part of the greenhouse was like, Daisy

couldn't wait to see the exotic flower emporium!

"And here is the emporium!" said the professor, opening a door marked 'Strictly Private'.

But no matter how hard she tried, Daisy couldn't hide her disappointment. She thought there'd be bigger and better specimens of the plants that she had successfully grown in Little Blossoming, but instead all she saw were shrivelled brown plants in desperate need of care and attention.

"Oh, the poor things," cried Daisy, rushing over to them.

"Oh, indeed," said the professor, trying to sound brave. "It's another little test, so I can get a better idea of what you already know."

Daisy nodded gravely, but she wasn't really listening. She was more

concerned with tending the flowers
as quickly as she could.

"Please can I borrow your phone?
I need to make an emergency call.
Time is not on our side, and without
the help of my friend, I don't think
these flowers will survive."

* * *

As soon as Felicity heard the news,
she packed a bag and took the
sleeper train to Floral Castle. When
she arrived the next day she headed
straight to the greenhouse, and found
Daisy fast asleep amongst the pots.

"Daisy, wake up," said Felicity,
gently stirring her friend. "I'm here to
help now."

"Oh, Felicity, what am I going to
do?" cried Daisy. "These poor flowers
have been neglected for so long. I
don't think they'll make it through
the day."

"With your Blossom Fairy care and

love, these flowers will soon be
blooming again. Just believe in
yourself," said Felicity, helping Daisy
to her feet.

* * *

The fairy friends worked tirelessly all
day. They talked, sang, stroked, and
gently tended the poorly plants with
all the love they could muster. By
the end of the day they had all the
exotic emporium flowers in a stable
condition.

"That's amazing," said Professor

Gushing, who could already see a difference in the plants. "Being a novice fairy you probably wouldn't know, but seeds from magical Mount Stamen are notoriously difficult to grow."

Daisy bit her lip and felt tears well up in her eyes. She felt deeply let down. She had looked up to Professor Gushing for years. She had always wanted to be like her, but now she realized she was nothing to be envied at all.

"How did I do?" said Daisy quietly.

"Do?" said Professor Gushing, staring into space.

"In the test?" prompted Daisy.

"Oh, yes, the test!" said Professor Gushing. "Um, ten out of ten."

"It's been a long day," said Felicity, leading her teary friend up the long staircase. "Let's go to bed, Daisy."

* * *

Felicity fell straight asleep, but Daisy was still tossing and turning. It had not turned out to be the course she'd imagined when she'd set off so excitedly from Little Blossoming.

Daisy switched on the bedside light, tiptoed out of bed and reached up to pull down one of Professor Gushing's books from the bookshelf.

"Daisy, what are you doing?" asked Felicity, halfasleep.

"I'm just going to read for a bit. Go back to sleep, Felicity," said Daisy, settling back into bed with the book.

"Wow," thought Daisy as she opened up the first pages. "A first edition – with a photo of the author." And she flicked through the pages she knew almost off by heart.

"You used to know it all, Professor," thought Daisy. "Maybe all Blossom Fairies become lazy and forget? Perhaps there is just too much information to remember! But how can you forget to love plants?"

Then Daisy saw the photo... and suddenly everything became clear.

* * *

The next morning, when Daisy had finished filling Felicity in on her late-night discovery, she decided she had a test of her own for Professor Gushing.

"So," said Daisy when they sat

down for breakfast. "When did you graduate, Professor?"

Felicity gave Daisy a smile of encouragement.

"Oh, a long time ago," said Professor Gushing, fidgeting in her seat.

"You can't remember the year?" said Daisy, determined not to give in. "It's a very important ceremony that no fairy ever forgets."

Professor Gushing looked awkward. "Oh, I haven't forgotten, I just can't remember at this precise moment. Um, do you fancy tending to the exotic plants again today?"

"You graduated from Seven Wish School, didn't you?" persisted Daisy.

"Oh, yes, it was a lovely school, wonderful, the best school in the world."

"I'm sure it would be... if it existed, Persephone!" said Daisy.

Suddenly the fairy that Daisy had known as Professor Gushing crumpled her wings, sat down on a chair and began to sob. She'd been caught!

"I didn't mean to lie to you," Persephone cried. "I didn't mean to lie to anyone. It was just that Professor Gushing was going away and all I wanted to do was have a lovely surprise here for her when she got back. I went to magical Mount Stamen, collected all the flowers and created the emporium myself, but I soon realized that there's more to being a Blossom Fairy than just a bit of water and sweet-talking. Professor Gushing is due back next week and when you came along I thought I'd found the answer to everything. Only, now you know…" And Persephone began to sob uncontrollably.

"I'm sure you've always been a very good assistant in every way, but you're not a Blossom Fairy," said Felicity, putting an arm around Persephone.

"No, I'm not," said Persephone. "I should never have deceived all those people, it was very wrong. And I've ruined everything!"

Daisy thought long and hard.

"Well, not quite everything. We've got one more day before we have to go back to school. If I show you step by step how to take care of the exotic flowers, so that Professor Gushing does have that lovely surprise when she returns, perhaps she might be in a good enough mood to keep that promise to talk at the School of Nine Wishes?"

"I'm sure she will be!" said Persephone, wiping away her tears. "I'll make sure of it!"

✷ ✷ ✷

When Daisy and Felicity met the real Professor Gushing for the first time it was just before she was about to go on stage at the School of Nine Wishes.

"I've heard a lot about you two," said Professor Gushing seriously. "It appears that the exotic flowers wouldn't exist without you, Daisy, and your friend Felicity Wishes. So it shall be called 'Daisy's Exotic Flower Emporium'. A true Blossom Fairy can open the buds of any plant with love, and you have shown your heart to be true. Thank you."

Daisy floated on a cloud of invisible petals all the way back to her seat.

"See," said Felicity to Daisy. "If you believe in your dreams, they *can* come true!"

If you really believe
in your dreams

they can come true

Emma Thomson's

felicity Wishes®

Winnie is sent on a

life changing adventure halfway

around Fairy World in

Winnie's Wonderland

Winnie's Wonderland

Even though Winnie hadn't been at the School of Nine Wishes for long, she no longer felt like a new girl. She had found best friends in Felicity Wishes, Holly, Polly and Daisy, and with them, exciting adventures made new memories each day.

When Felicity and her friends first met Winnie she was shy, quiet, and even a little nervous. But one day she went on a life-changing adventure halfway around Fairy World, and she was never quite the same fairy again...

✳ ✳ ✳

It was the end of term at the School of Nine Wishes. Although Winnie had made some good friends, Miss Meandering, her form tutor, had noticed that she was still rather shy and sometimes didn't have the confidence to join in with the other fairies. Miss Meandering was sure that there was a more adventurous spirit hiding behind Winnie's shyness.

"Where's Winnie?" asked Felicity, playing leapfrog with Daisy and Polly in the playground at break-time.

"Miss Meandering asked her to stay behind after class," said Polly.

"Oh, I hope she isn't in trouble," said Felicity, landing with a bump.

"You know I'm not one for gossip," said Holly, smiling. "But I've heard a rumour that Miss Meandering is going to ask Winnie to represent the School of Nine Wishes on a visit to our sister school."

"But that doesn't sound like Winnie!" gasped Felicity. "You know she's happiest at home with her close friends."

"Well, almost all gossip starts with something true," said Holly with a wink.

* * *

And the rumour about Winnie was true; only a week later, Felicity and her friends were waving Winnie off on her trip to an island on the other side of Fairy World.

"Promise to write to us," said Felicity, feeling a little teary. She was going to miss her new friend. "I've packed you some chocolate hearts for the journey!"

"And here's a spare pair of tights," said Holly. "Just in case!"

Polly and Daisy gave Winnie presents too. Polly had wrapped up an emergency torch and Daisy gave Winnie a photo of all five of them at

Glitter Beach last weekend.

"You're the best friends a fairy could ever have!" called Winnie. "I promise I'll write to you every week!"

The four fairy friends waved frantically as Winnie flew off with a huge bag on her shoulders, a map in one hand and a compass in the other.

Winnie had never been anywhere so far away from home before. Every time she thought of the journey ahead, her tummy would flutter, but she wasn't quite sure whether it was because of nerves or excitement. It was going to be a long journey, but an exciting adventure that she would never forget.

✳ ✳ ✳

"Have you heard from Winnie yet?" Polly asked Felicity when the fairy friends met up at Sparkles Café the following weekend.

"No, not yet. It's been a week since she left and I don't even know if she has made it to her destination," said Felicity anxiously.

"Don't worry, Felicity. I'm sure she will be fine," said Daisy, trying to reassure herself as much as Felicity.

* * *

A long week later, Felicity heard the clatter of her letter box and fluttered downstairs as fast as her wings could carry her. There on the mat was what she had been waiting for – a postcard from Winnie!

My fairy friends, Felicity, Holly, Polly and Daisy,

Sorry for not writing before. Our boat sank! Please don't worry. I got everyone off safely. Should reach our sister school very soon and will write more when I can.

Love and wishes,
Winnie xx

To
Felicity Wishes

Little Blossoming,
Near Bloomfield

Felicity looked at the card, perplexed, and then slowly read it again.

* * *

"That's nice," said Holly at school later that day, scanning the postcard and flipping it over to look at the picture of a beach hotel on the front.

Felicity raised her eyebrows.

"Read it again!" she urged Holly. "Would you say that postcard came from a shy, quiet and nervous fairy?"

Daisy peeped over Holly's shoulder at the postcard. "No way!" said Daisy. "You wouldn't get a nervous fairy rescuing everyone from a sinking boat!"

"That's exactly what I thought!" said Felicity.

* * *

Felicity's tiny concerns grew into huge worries when she received Winnie's next postcard, a few days later.

My fairy friends, Felicity,
   Holly, Polly and Daisy,

Got here safely. Everyone is lovely.
I gave the school a speech about
our little town and now they all
want to come and visit!
      Love and wishes,
         Winnie xx

To
Felicity Wishes
Little
Blossoming,
Near Bloomfield

Felicity had begun to suspect that it wasn't Winnie writing the postcards, but someone else!

Read the rest of

Emma Thomson's
felicity Wishes®

Winnie's Wonderland

to find out what
has happened to Winnie...

If you enjoyed this book, why not try another of these fantastic story collections?

Designer Drama

Star Surprise

Clutter Clean-out

Newspaper Nerves

Enchanted Escape

Whispering Wishes

8

Friends Forever

7

Sensational Secrets

9

Happy Hobbies

11

Wand Wishes

10

Party Pickle

12

Dancing Dreams

13 Spooky Sleepover

14 Fashion Fiasco

15 Pink Paradise

16 Spectacular Skies

17 Dreamy Daisy

18 Perfect Polly

WOULD YOU LIKE TO BE A FRIEND OF FELICITY?

Felicity Wishes has her very own website,
filled with lots of sparkly fairy fun and information
about Felicity Wishes and all her fairy friends.

Just visit:

www.felicitywishes.net

to find out all about
Felicity's books,
sign up to
competitions,
quizzes and
special offers.

And if you want
to show how much
you love your friends,
you can even send
them a Felicity e-card
for free. It will truly
brighten up their day!

For full terms and conditions visit www.felicitywishes.net/terms

SEE YOUR FRIENDSHIP LETTER HERE!

Write in and tell us all about your best friend, and you could see your letter published in one of the Felicity Wishes' books.

Please send in your letter, including your name and age with a stamped self-addressed envelope to:

Felicity Wishes Friendship Competition

Hodder Children's Books, 338 Euston Road, London NW1 3BH

Australian readers should write to...
Hachette Children's Books
Level 17/207 Kent Street, Sydney, NSW 2000, Australia

New Zealand readers should write to...
Hachette Children's Books
PO Box 100-749 North Shore Mail Centre, Auckland, New Zealand

Closing date is 30 April 2007

ALL ENTRIES MUST BE SIGNED BY A PARENT OR GUARDIAN.
TO BE ELIGIBLE ENTRANTS MUST BE UNDER 13 YEARS.

For full terms and conditions visit www.felicitywishes.net/terms

Friends of Felicity

Dear Felicinty Wishes,

I would like to nomanate my best friend Scarlett. She is my best friend becuse she makes me laugh soooo much. She very kind she goes Austraiia about 16 times a year and allways bring me somthing back. She is my best friend because she could have picked anyone else in my class but she picked me!!!

lot of love
from abi

x x x x x x x x x
x x x x x x
x x x x x
x x x x
x x x
x x
x

WIN FELICITY WISHES PRIZES!

From January 2006, there will
be a Felicity Wishes fiction book
publishing each month (in Australia
and New Zealand publishing from
April 2006) with a different
sticker on each cover. Collect
all twelve stickers and stick
them on the collectors' card which
you'll find in Dancing Dreams or
download from www.felicitywishes.net

Send in your completed card to the relevant
address below and you'll be entered into a
grand prize draw to receive a Felicity Wishes prize.*

Felicity Wishes Collectors' Competition

Hodder Children's Books, 338 Euston Road, London NW1 3BH

Australian readers should write to...
Hachette Children's Books
Level 17/207 Kent Street, Sydney, NSW 2000, Australia

New Zealand readers should write to...
Hachette Children's Books
PO Box 100-749 North Shore Mail Centre, Auckland, New Zealand

*A draw to pick 50 winners each month
will take place from January 2007 – 30 June 2007.

For full terms and conditions visit www.felicitywishes.net/terms